For all children

With special thanks to Saied Shahsavari
for inspiration and support

Illustrated by Ghazal Barati

www.callymacdonald.com

I Feel Good Because ...

Everyone is Happy

Cally MacDonald

There was a knock on the door.
TAP TAP TAP
Emma and Teddy looked surprised.

"*Who could that be?*" Teddy said.
"Ssshhh, nobody knows you talk to me except Mum," Emma said.

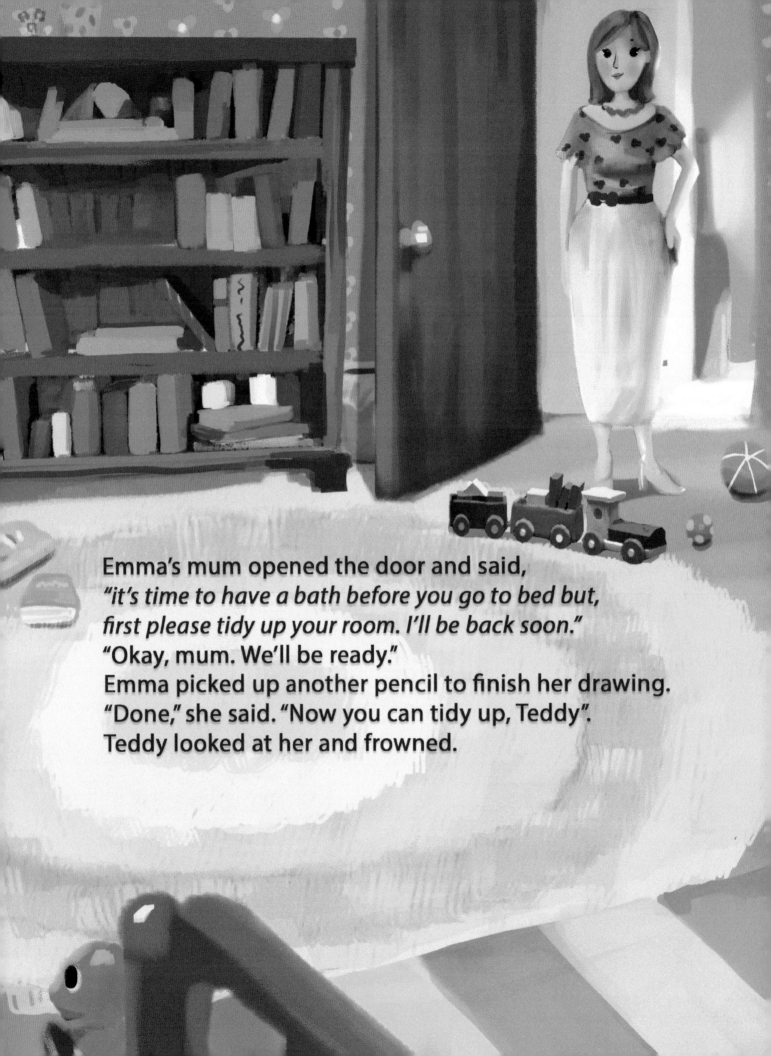

Emma's mum opened the door and said,
"it's time to have a bath before you go to bed but,
first please tidy up your room. I'll be back soon."
"Okay, mum. We'll be ready."
Emma picked up another pencil to finish her drawing.
"Done," she said. "Now you can tidy up, Teddy".
Teddy looked at her and frowned.

Emma's mum ran a big hot bath full of bubbles. Emma could hardly be seen.
"*I know you enjoy the bath but, you didn't tidy up your room.*"
"I wanted to tidy up my room but, Teddy was too tired." Emma replied.

"Oh, I see. Would you like me to help you and Teddy tidy up before you go to sleep?"
"I would but, Teddy likes us to do it together."
"Oh, okay." Her mum smiled.

Emma and Teddy were lying in bed in their pyjamas when Emma said, "are you awake?"
"Yes," Teddy replied. "*Can I ask you something?*" he said.
"*Would you go to sleep if I was unhappy and lying on the floor?*"

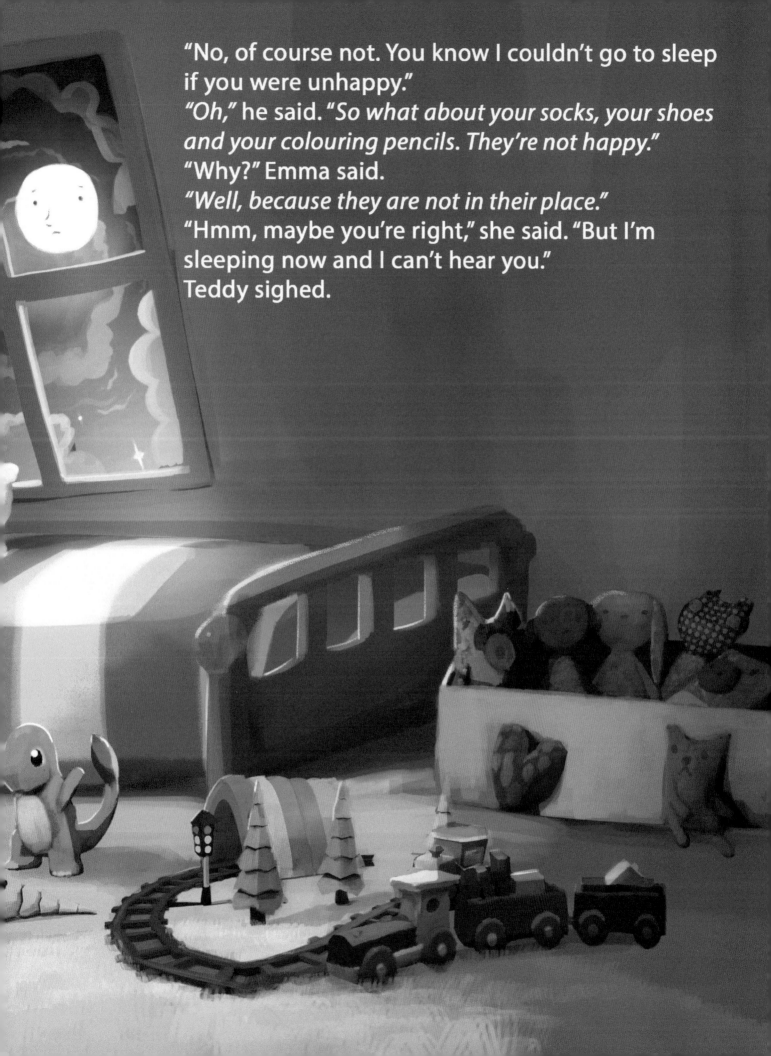

"No, of course not. You know I couldn't go to sleep if you were unhappy."

"Oh," he said. *"So what about your socks, your shoes and your colouring pencils. They're not happy."*

"Why?" Emma said.

"Well, because they are not in their place."

"Hmm, maybe you're right," she said. "But I'm sleeping now and I can't hear you."

Teddy sighed.

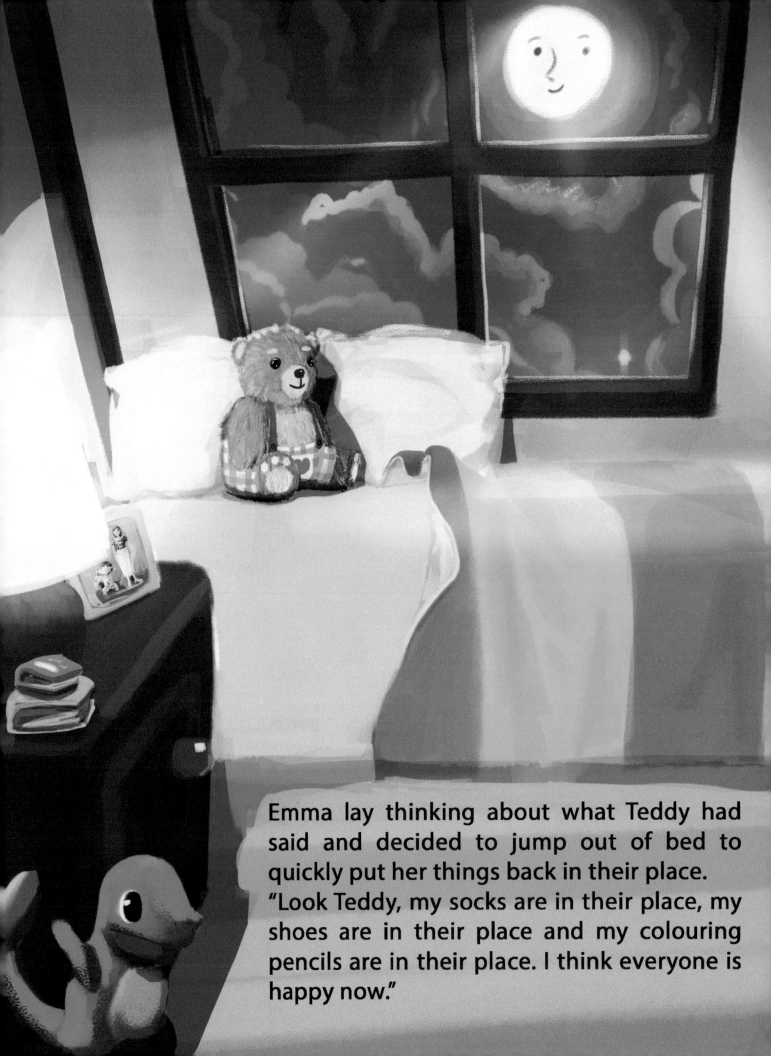

Emma lay thinking about what Teddy had said and decided to jump out of bed to quickly put her things back in their place. "Look Teddy, my socks are in their place, my shoes are in their place and my colouring pencils are in their place. I think everyone is happy now."

"Yes, I agree. We can all be truly happy when everyone is happy," Teddy said.

Emma was so sleepy and climbed back into bed.
She yawned and said, "ahhh-haaa, Teddy, I love you so
much and I feel good because everyone is happy."
"I love you too and now we are all ready to go to sleep."

"Recorderrr, recorderrr, recorderrr."
"What are you doing?"
"I am trying to wake you up with music but,
I couldn't find my recorder."
"That's not music... and you couldn't find it
because it wasn't in its place."

TAP TAP TAP

Emma's mum knocked on the door and popped her head into the room. *"Good morning, Emma"* she said looking around. *"Wow, how tidy your room is. You've both been busy."*

"Yes, Teddy and I couldn't sleep until everyone was happy."

"Oh, so when things are in their place they are happy?"

"Yes, they are."

"Well done to you and Teddy. I am so impressed. Breakfast will be ready soon so please wash your hands and face and come to the table."

Emma's mum had made a lovely breakfast and everything was ready and in its place.
"What do you think of the table? Is everything happy?"
"Yes, they are."
"After breakfast, we'll all get dressed and go out. I want to take you and Teddy somewhere to show you something."
Emma and Teddy clapped with excitement.

As Emma's mum was helping her to put on her shoes she said, *"you and Teddy did so well last night."*
Emma leaned forward and whispered, "are you happy?"
"Of course, when everyone is happy, I'm happy too."
Emma smiled and said, "you know mum, when you are happy I feel good."

Printed in Great Britain
by Amazon

79677017R00016